Millie Cooper's Ride

A True Story from History

by Marc Simmons
Illustrations by Ronald Kil

UNIVERSITY OF NEW MEXICO PRESS
ALBUQUERQUE

Library of Congress Cataloging-in-Publication Data
Simmons, Marc.
Millie Cooper's ride : a true story from history / by Marc Simmons ;
illustrations by Ronald R. Kil.
p. cm.
Summary: During the War of 1812, when settlers at Fort Cooper, Missouri,
are besieged by a coalition of Indian nations allied with the British, twelve-year-old
Millie volunteers to ride to nearby Fort Hempstead for reinforcements.
ISBN 0-8263-2925-X (alk. paper)
1. Cooper, Millie—Juvenile fiction. 2. United States—History—War of 1812—Juvenile
fiction. [1. Cooper, Millie—Fiction. 2. United States—History—War of 1812—Fiction.
3. Missouri—History—19th century—Fiction. 4. Indians of North America—Fiction.]
I. Kil, Ronald R., 1959–   ill. II. Title.
PZ7.S591855 Mi 2002
[Fic—dc21]   2002002853
Printed in Singapore

for Corrina Kil
who is something of a "Millie" herself

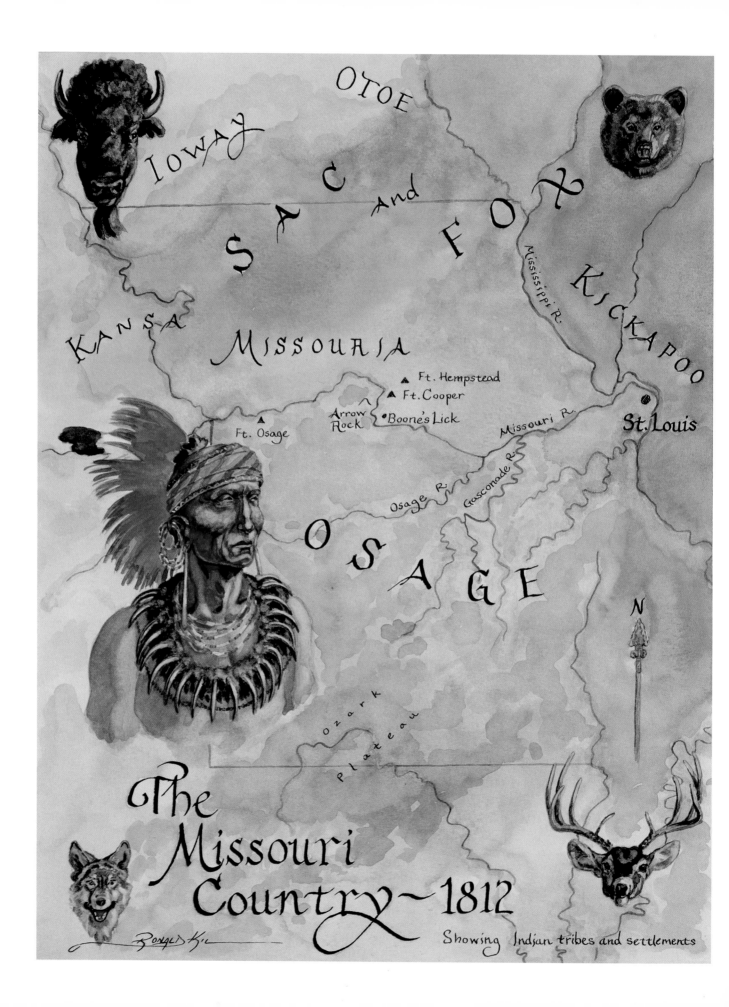

Foreword

T HE events in this story took place in the wild Boone's Lick country of central Missouri. They happened during the War of 1812, when the United States was fighting Great Britain. The British attacked America's seacoast. But they also sent their agents to stir up Indian tribes on the frontier and persuade them to attack American settlers.

In 1810, Colonel Benjamin Cooper, with his family, led 150 people to the salt spring, or lick, named for pioneer Daniel Boone. A few miles away, they cleared land for farming in the Missouri River bottoms. And some of them built a log stockade called Fort Cooper, for protection. Others moved into the uplands six miles east and built Fort Hempstead.

What follows is an amazing tale about these hardy Americans, and about a small girl among them who showed great courage.

MILLIE Cooper was not happy. It was her twelfth birthday, and her parents expected her to work just like any ordinary day. When dawn broke, she had no thought that before nightfall swift events would be pushing her in the direction of a chilling adventure.

At the plank breakfast table that morning, Millie hungrily gobbled down her bowl of corn mush. It was sweetened with wild honey. Her older brother David had harvested it from a hollow bee tree.

But even the tasty honey did not improve her mood. Birthdays ought to be a special event, she decided. Yet, no one inside Fort Cooper had time to spend on such foolishness. There was too much work to be done. So even a child's birthday had to be put aside.

After she washed her bowl and spoon, Mille went outside. She gazed over the busy activity in the center of the fort, and her spirits rose.

Some of the men were hitching up their plow mules. Others were checking their long rifles for the day's hunting. Adam Woods saddled his horse, intending to ride over to the lick for a sack of salt. His wife had told him that her salt bin in their kitchen was almost empty.

Millie noticed several women lined up at the well. They lowered buckets on a rope and drew up water for their households. It was laundry day, so extra water would be needed.

ITH a sinking heart, Millie realized that her mother would soon be calling her to stir the steaming laundry tubs with a hickory stick. That was not a chore the birthday girl liked to think about.

Luckily, she was rescued by her friend Jane Alcorn.

"Come on Millie," invited Jane. "Let's go to the work shed. The boys cut nettles along the river yesterday. So we have a fresh stack to peel."

That sounded easier to Millie Cooper than washing clothes. Nettle fibers taken from the stems could be pulled and twisted into lengths of heavy thread. Both Millie and Jane regularly wore simple nettle dresses. That shows just how poor the Fort Cooper folk were in those early days.

Young David Cooper passed by the shed. "You girls sure enough got an easy life working in this shade," he said smiling. Then he walked on.

"Don't you pay him any mind," Millie advised Jane. "He just likes to tease me, and he still pulls my pigtails. Now that I'm twelve, father must tell him to leave my hair alone."

About then, both girls heard a noise. *Baa-aa.*

"That sounds like a lost sheep," said Jane. "Or a lamb."

Millie went to the stockade and peered out through a hole between the logs. "It *is* a lamb," she replied. "It must have wandered away from somebody's flock."

Turning, Millie ran along the inside of the wall of the fort until she came to a small gate. Taking down the wooden bar, she opened the gate and slipped outside.

T HE lamb, Millie saw, was hungry, dirty, and had grass burs in its wool. When Jane ran up behind her, Millie said, "We better catch the poor thing and pen it up. Then we can look for the owner."

Jane felt sorry for the animal, too. But more than that, she was worried. "We're not supposed to go outside the fort alone, Millie. You know that. The grownups say it's too dangerous."

"Well, I'll grab the lamb and we'll go right back," Millie answered.

The skinny lamb, however, had other ideas. As the girls drew near, it raced away across the plowed fields. Without thinking, Millie sped after it.

Jane was a year older than Millie, but she couldn't run as fast. When she caught up with her friend, Millie had stopped in the middle of the open field. She was watching a flock of sheep an older boy had just driven out of the trees.

The lamb headed straight for the flock, and Millie knew it would find its mother. All was well!

Breathing hard from the run, an irritated Jane said, "This is just like you, Millie. You're always trying to help. But you just get us into trouble or put us in harm's way."

Millie paid no attention. Instead, she exclaimed, "Jane look over yonder!"

She was pointing to one of the fort's sentinels, or guardsmen, stationed at the edge of the woods. Like all sentinels, he carried a hollow cow's horn that he blew at the first sign of Indians.

"We're safe while he is keeping watch," Millie reminded Jane. And she added, "Come on. Let's hurry back. Maybe no one will notice we've been gone."

DURING the girls' absence, the quiet scene inside Fort Cooper had changed. Returning through the small rear gate, Millie and Jane saw that all was astir. People were dashing about or talking in small groups.

At first the children thought their short disappearance might have caused the uproar. But when Millie's mother rushed up, they learned that it was something more serious.

"I've been looking for you two," Mrs. Cooper blurted. "Mr. Woods brought word from the lick that Indians killed two Fort Hempstead men. Millie, your father has sent out scouts to see if the war party is still lurking about."

After sending Jane to find her own mother, Mrs. Cooper took daughter Millie by the hand and they went straight to their cabin.

That evening at the supper table, Colonel Cooper said to his wife, "The situation looks bad for us. I fear this is the beginning of many bloody attacks upon our people."

"Oh, mercy. I pray that isn't true," replied Mrs. Cooper.

"Most of the tribes have been friendly toward us," continued the Colonel. "But now the British are urging them to make war on the settlements. The Osage will stay on our side, but I'm sure that the Sacs and Foxes, Ioways, Otoes, and Kickapoos will not. Dark days lie ahead," he concluded.

Later when Millie crawled into her straw bed, pictures of the day's events filled her head. She scarcely remembered that it had been her birthday, as she dropped into a restless sleep.

URING the following weeks, Colonel Cooper's grim
prediction proved true. Men alone out hunting, fishing,
or farming fell victim to feathered arrows. Grazing horses and
cattle began to disappear.

One day a boatman coming up the Missouri River brought
Millie's father a letter from St. Louis. It was written by the
governor of the territory.

The letter warned Colonel Cooper that the Boone's Lick
country was in grave danger. Many tribes were joining together.
And British officers were urging them to attack Fort Cooper.

The Colonel was told that the American government could
not protect the settlers. So he was ordered to bring them all
down river to St. Louis for safety.

Millie listened as her father read the letter to the residents of the fort.

"Must we give up without a fight?" cried some of the men, angrily.

"We can't abandon our cabins and fields," protested others.

"We'll never leave!" shouted the whole crowd.

Thus Colonel Cooper wrote this reply to the governor in St. Louis:

> *Sir:*
>
> *We have made our homes here and it would ruin us to leave now. We are good Americans and have 200 men and boys who will fight to the last. And we have 100 women and girls who will take their places when they fall.*
>
> *Just send us gunpowder and lead for bullets. That's all we ask.*
>
> *Col. Cooper*

His words meant this: If the government cannot protect us, we will do the job ourselves.

THE wooden barrels of gunpowder and bars of lead for bullet making did not arrive. But the Indians did.

Two weeks had passed. One morning Millie and Jane climbed a ladder to a walkway on the inside walls. They were looking over the valley when suddenly from far down the river came the mournful bellow of a sentinel's horn.

Another horn, this one closer, picked up the call. Then a third, closer still. The girls bit their lips and turned pale. The war was coming to them.

Soon Millie and Jane were joined on the walls by others. They watched the last farmers hurrying in, driving what livestock they could find. Finally, their sentinels reached the fort and the heavy gate swung shut.

In the late morning heat, the people waited in silence. Millie felt the sweat trickle down her neck. Then she heard the drums, a kind of rolling thunder: boom, boom, BOOM!

Before long the grand Indian army came in sight.

THE Indians moved up the bottoms toward Fort Cooper. Men next to Millie called out the names of tribes they recognized. There were even some Shawnees from the far Ohio Valley.

"I see at least 500 warriors," declared Millie's brother, David.

The view of the native army was colorful to behold, but also terrifying. "Women and children must leave the walls," Colonel Cooper announced.

Only those needed as loaders did not go. Most of the men had two single-shot long rifles. In a fight, their sons stood alongside and loaded while they fired.

Millie went below with her mother to begin making bandages and have them ready for the wounded. But David Cooper remained on the walkway to load for the colonel. Mr. Alcorn had no son, so Jane also stayed behind as his loader.

The settlers expected an attack at once, but the Indians had other ideas. First, they lined up and shook their weapons in the air to show how strong and numerous they were. Then they withdrew into the thick belt of trees behind them.

At first Colonel Cooper was puzzled by that. "Why aren't they attacking?" he thought to himself. But in a few minutes he said to Mr. Woods standing nearby: "That Indian army has decided to have lunch and maybe take a nap in the hot afternoon. They think we can be easily conquered, so they're in no hurry."

MILLIE'S father now called a council of the men in the center of the fort. Behind them crowded the women and children, listening.

"There's little hope for us," Colonel Cooper told them. "In a few hours, the enemy will overrun our walls and we will all die fighting."

"Our only chance," said the colonel softly, "is to send someone through the Indian lines to Fort Hempstead. Perhaps our neighbors will come to our relief."

That anyone could survive such a daring ride seemed impossible. Men and boys looked at the ground. They were afraid. No one volunteered.

Then, Millie Cooper nervously stepped into the open circle and said: "Let me go, father. I'll try."

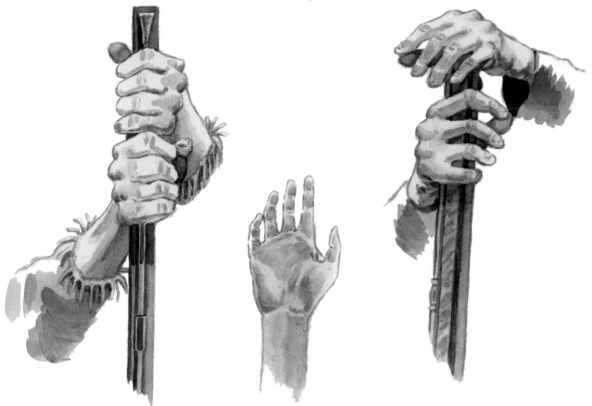

With a sorrowful heart, Colonel Cooper agreed. His daughter was not needed on the walls during the coming fight. She could be spared.

"Bring a horse," someone yelled. From the fort corral a young animal named Star was led forward.

Benjamin Cooper saddled the horse. He lifted his daughter onto its back, asking, "Is there any last thing you want, Millie?"

"Just a spur, father," she replied.

So a small spur was sent for and the colonel tied it to her left foot.

Then the men opened the gate. Millie kicked with her spur and Star sprang into action. Everyone raced to the walkway to watch.

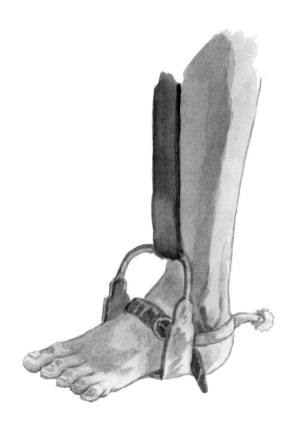

T HE road to Fort Hempstead ran through plowed ground, heading straight for the woods at the edge of the uplands. As her horse stretched into a run, Millie bent low in the saddle. Her pigtails blew straight back from her head. Folks in the fort could see her left leg rising and falling as she worked that spur.

Upon entering the thick trees, Millie disappeared from the settlers' view. Her father had been right. The Indians were busy eating and napping.

The girl and her racing horse suddenly burst through some Kickapoos roasting meat. Flying hoofs scattered their campfire.

Frightened as she was, Millie kept going. The Indians shot arrows, fired old British muskets, and sounded war whoops. While the arrows and bullets missed, a tree branch struck Millie on the side of the head. But she hardly noticed.

Then Millie broke free of the woods and found the road again to Fort Hempstead. The Kickapoos, who were on foot, could not follow her.

"Please, Star," the girl begged, "please get me to the fort!"

Millie was dizzy now and afraid of falling off her horse. A big bump swelled on her head where the tree branch hit her.

"I must keep going," she groaned.

All things around her grew blurry. Millie could hardly see the road. Yet, she pushed on.

An hour later, clinging to the saddle, Millie Cooper glimpsed Fort Hempstead far ahead. Then her eyes closed and all went dark.

BACK at Fort Cooper, the settlers were awaiting the attack. They had seen their little messenger plunge into the trees. Then they heard the war whoops and gunshots, followed by silence. A feeling of dread and despair spread throughout the fort.

Jane on the walkway said to her father: "Oh! My friend Millie has fallen and is gone."

"I'm afraid so, my dear," Mr. Alcorn replied sadly. "There will be no help for us now. We are all doomed."

Hours later, the sun dipped low in the west. The shadows grew long and the drums began again. The whole Indian army emerged from the trees for the storming of the fort.

It started with Indian bowmen shooting swarms of arrows arching into the air. Some thudded into the log walls. Other arrows fell inside the fort, hitting people and animals.

As Jane loaded her father's rifle, a boy next to her was struck in the shoulder and fell from the walkway. All the men fired rapidly. Thick clouds of gunsmoke soon blackened their faces.

Although arrows whizzed by her ears like bees, Jane paid attention only to her loading. Through the smoke, she glimpsed hundreds of Indians moving toward the walls.

As she poured more gunpowder into the rifle barrel, Jane said to herself, "This is the end."

But it was not the end. Miraculously, the Indian army that had been surging forward suddenly stopped in its tracks.

Surprised, the settlers ceased firing their rifles. "Listen!" Colonel Cooper shouted. "Do you hear that?" Jane stopped her loading and listened.

There on the evening air came the sweet sound of popping long rifles from the uplands behind the trees. "Help has arrived from Fort Hempstead!" yelled Jane's father.

The Indians saw that they were caught between two lines of gunfire, front and back. So the attackers broke off the fight and fled up the Missouri Valley.

Jane's heart rejoiced. Millie Cooper had made it through after all!

For a few minutes, the men and women of Fort Cooper stood speechless, so stunned were they by the turn of events. They had been prepared to die. Now they were saved.

Finally, several women fell on their knees to shout, "Glory be!" and to give thanks. They hugged their children while the menfolk cheered.

"Open the gate!" Colonel Cooper commanded loudly.

Men rushed to comply. Joyously, they flung the gate wide open, eager to welcome their neighbors from Fort Hempstead.

The first person to enter was Millie, looking small on her lathered horse and wearing a huge bandage on her head.

At first, she was dazed by the large crowd surrounding her. But then she saw Jane, whose face was blackened by gunsmoke.

Suddenly, both girls were smiling, and Millie exclaimed, "Jane, you look like you fell down a sooty chimney." For the first time that terrible day, the two of them laughed.

Isaac Clark, a leader of the Fort Hempstead party, rode in right behind Millie.

"This daughter of yours is mighty brave," he told Millie's parents.

There was not a person inside Fort Cooper who could argue with that.

An Afterword

In 1819 a Mr. A. Fuller, new resident of the Boone's Lick country, wrote to his friend, Tom, who remained back East. "The residents here," he said, "are still talking about the daughter of Colonel Cooper. A few years ago when the fort was attacked, she volunteered to dash through the Indians and bring help. And she got back in time to save her friends."

"I'll tell you, Tom, there is an independence and nobleness in the faces of these young folks, dressed in their home-made clothing."

Peace with the Indians soon came. Mildred (Millie) Cooper grew up and married a farmer, Robert Brown. The story of her heroic act became part of the folk history of central Missouri.

It was related to children around the fireplace on long winter nights. The tale reminded youngsters of the importance of doing their duty toward family and country. And it taught them the value of courage.

As for Millie Cooper Brown, however, that childhood experience stayed with her as a horrifying memory, one she would have liked to forget.

So far as we know, she never spoke to others about her gallant ride.